A LONG WAY AWAY

LB

Little, Brown and Company
New York · Boston

AUG 14 2013

Little, Brown and Company

Hachette Book Group
237 Park Avenue, New York, NY 10017
Visit our website at www.lb-kids.com

Little, Brown and Company is a division of Hachette Book Group, Inc.
The Little, Brown name and logo are trademarks of Hachette Book Group, Inc.

The publisher is not responsible for websites (or their content) that are not owned by the publisher.

Library of Congress Cataloging-in-Publication Data

Viva, Frank.
A long way away / Frank Viva.—1st ed.
p. cm.
Summary: "A picture book that can be read front-to-back or back-to-front.
Start from one end and journey from outer space down to the sea;
start from the other end and journey from deep in the sea out to a distant planet"
—Provided by publisher.
ISBN 978-0-316-22196-2 (hc)
1. Upside-down books—Specimens. [1. Outer space—Fiction.
2. Interplanetary voyages—Fiction.
3. Ocean—Fiction. 4. Upside-down books.] I. Title.
PZ7.V827Lon 2013
[E]—dc23
2012028757

10 9 8 7 6 5 4 3 2 · IM · Printed in China

P9-CKU-776

A HUG

A HAPPY FACE

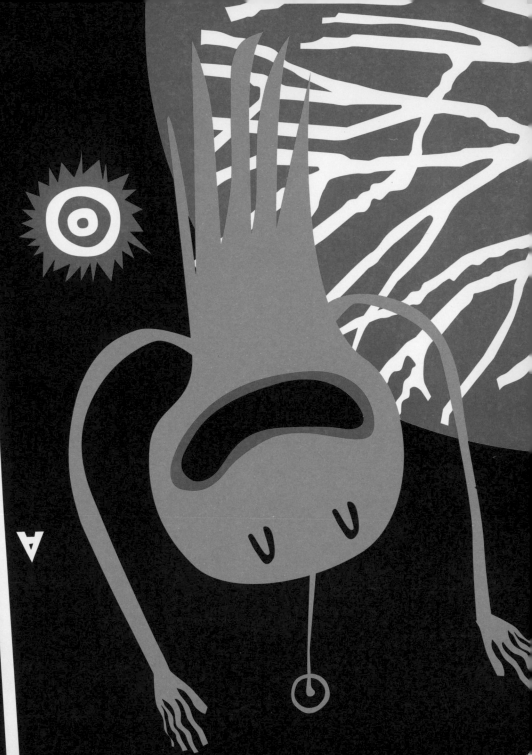

A HAPPY PLACE

A LONG WAY

AWAY

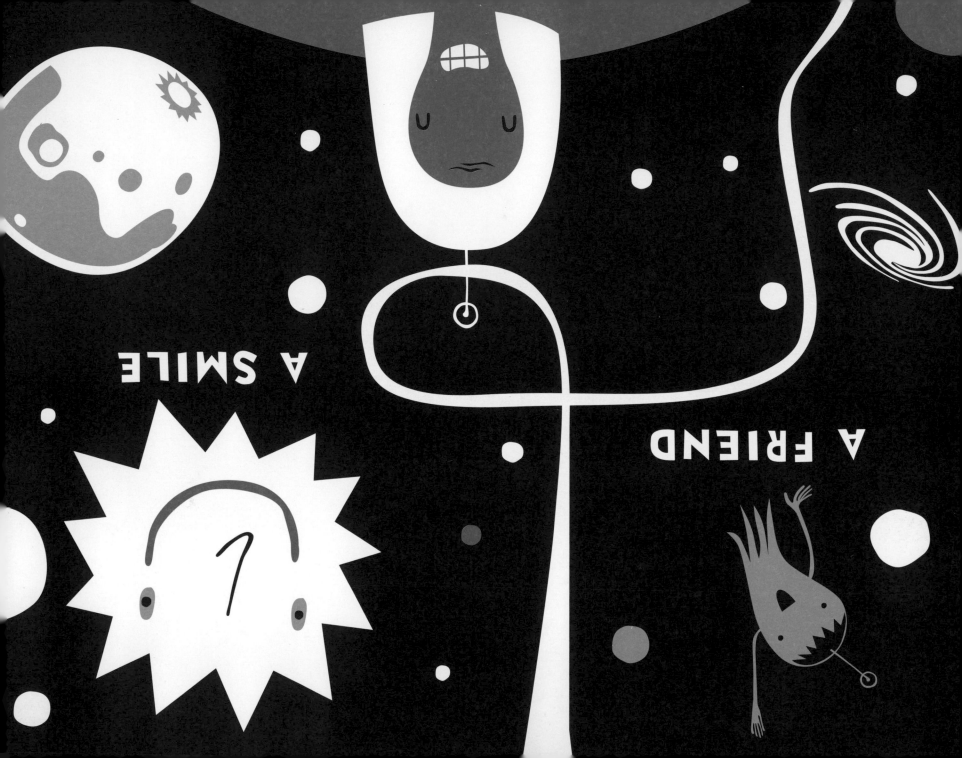

ZOOMING

AROUND

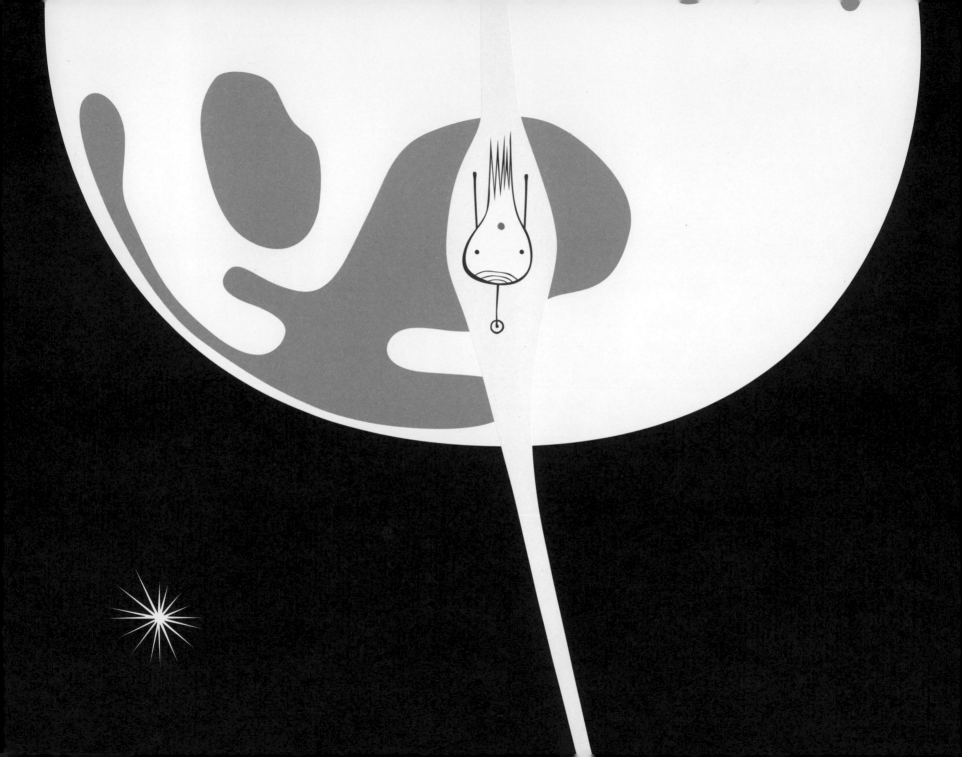

THE MOON IS A BALLOON

THIS AWAY

THAT AWAY

AND FAR BELOW

A LAGOON

ICE CREAM

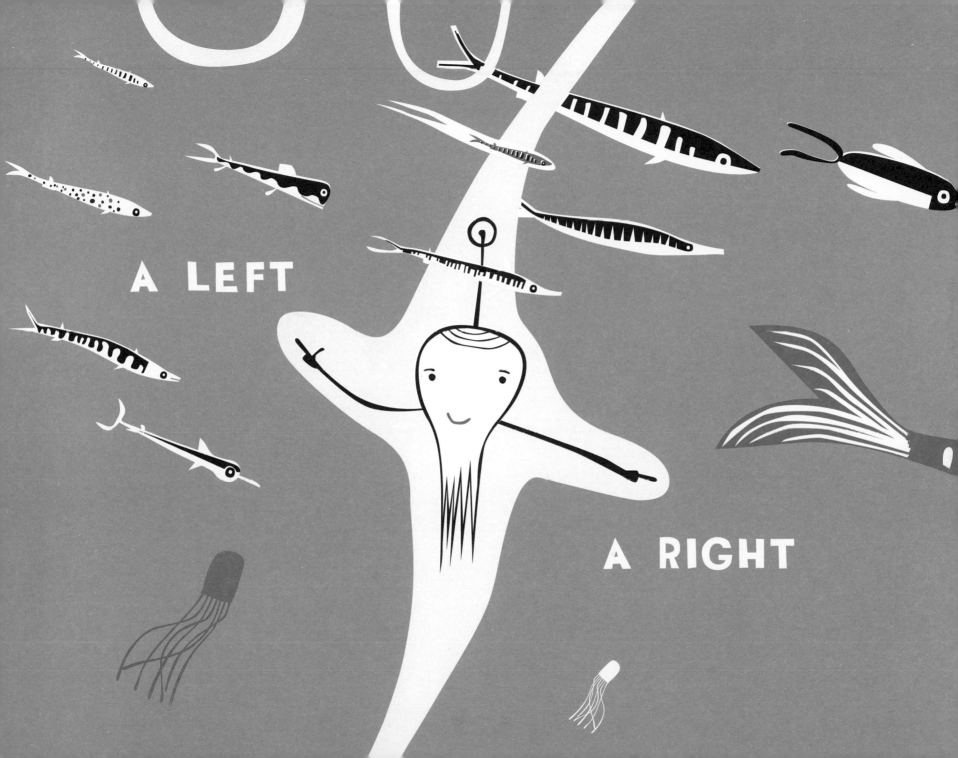

A LEFT

A RIGHT

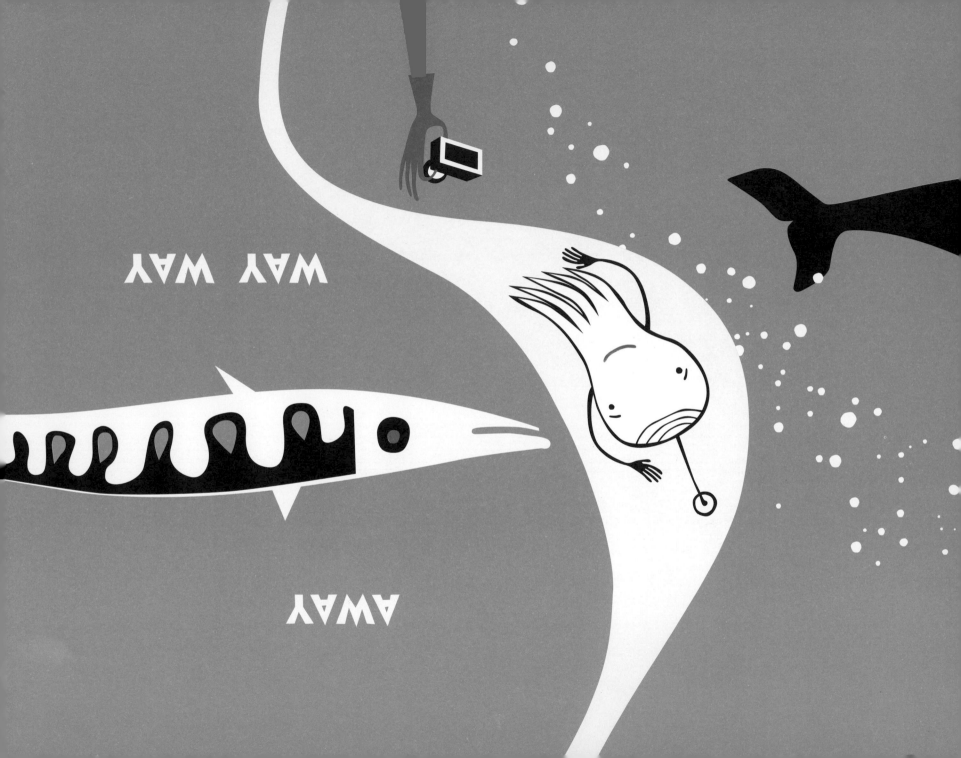

AND AWAY

GETTING READY

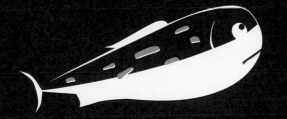

STEADY

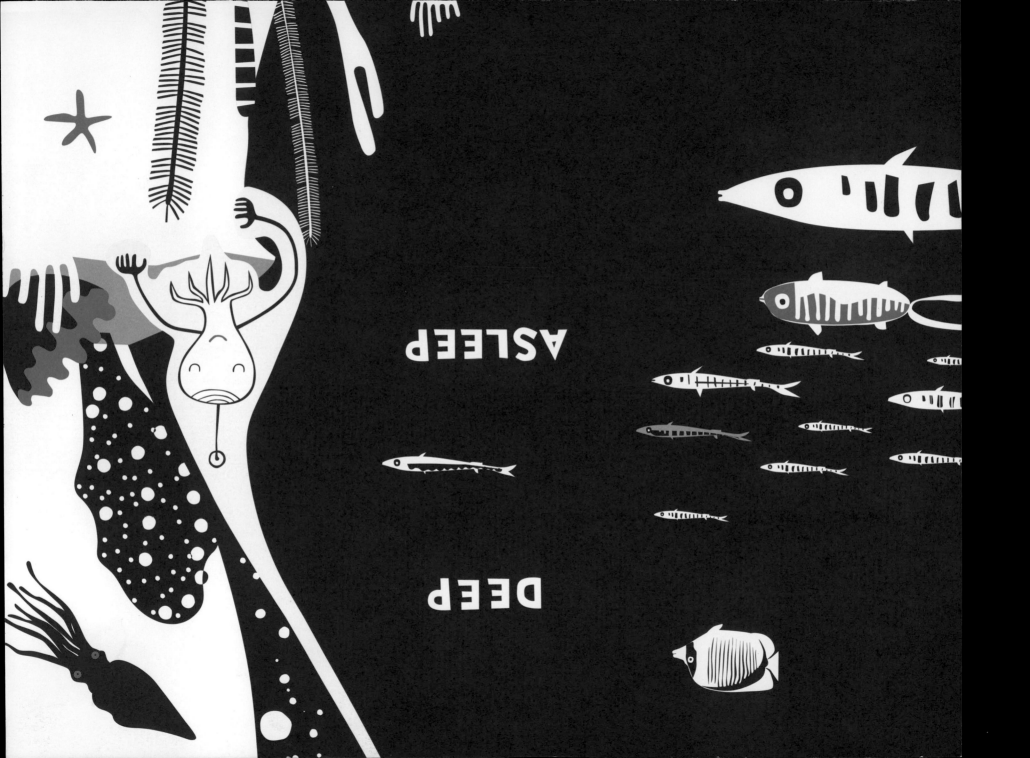

A LONG WAY AWAY

Ⓛ Ⓑ

Little, Brown and Company
New York • Boston

Frank Viva likes to travel up and down and up and down. He is a *New Yorker* cover artist, an award-winning designer, and the creator of the *New York Times* Best Illustrated Children's Book *Along a Long Road*.

FOR
MOM
+
DAD

A Long Way Away was created as a single, continuous twenty-six-foot-long piece of art using Adobe Illustrator. It was printed on 140gsm Gold Sun Woodfree paper. The type was hand drawn by Frank Viva (the cover title type is based on Neutraface). This book was edited by Susan Rich and designed by Saho Fujii and Frank Viva under the art direction of Patti Ann Harris. The production was supervised by Charlotte Veaney, and the production editor was Barbara Bakowski.